MAX
AND THE
BIG FAT LIE
A BOOK ABOUT
TELLING THE TRUTH

Michael P. Waite
Illustrated by Gary Trousdale

Chariot Books
David C. Cook Publishing Co.

For my nieces, Mari and Hannah. *MPW*

To my friends and family and loved ones
and, of course, to the people with the good
sense to buy this book. *GAT*

Chariot Books is an imprint of David C. Cook Publishing Co.
David C. Cook Publishing Co., Elgin, Illinois 60120
David C. Cook Publishing Co., Weston, Ontario
MAX AND THE BIG FAT LIE
© 1988 by Michael P. Waite for text and illustrations

Cover design by Dawn Lauck
First printing, 1988
Printed in the United States of America
93 92 91 90   5 4 3

Library of Congress Cataloging-in-Publication Data

Waite, Michael P.
      Max and the Big Fat Lie
      (Building Christian character series)
      Summary: Max feels bad after he lies to his mother in order to see a scary movie. Includes a related Bible verse.
      [1. Honesty—Fiction. 2. Christian life—Fiction. 3. Stories in rhyme] I. Trousdale, Gary, ill. II. Title. III. Series: Waite,
Michael P.
Building Christian character series.
PZ8.3.W136Max 1988   [E]   87-35511
ISBN 1-55513-617-6

Dear Mom and Dad,

Did you ever hide your child's pill in a spoonful of jelly? That's how the lesson about telling the truth is tucked into *Max and the Big Fat Lie*. The teaching is couched in a fun, rhyming story.

You and your children can't help but smile at Max and his ever-growing lies. But there's no missing his message: Telling the truth is always better than lying.

How can you use this book to help train your children?

Read *Max and the Big Fat Lie* aloud, as a family. Talk about the story and why telling the truth is important for God's children. Discuss Proverbs 12:22, the verse found on page 31, and memorize it together. The verse will serve as a reminder of the Christian character trait of telling the truth.

Use catch words from the story to remind each other of the lesson: "Remember Max's big fat lie" may become your family's code for "remember to tell the truth."

Young readers will enjoy reading the book to themselves and to their younger brothers and sisters. Nonreaders can tell themselves the story by looking at the pictures after it's been read aloud a couple of times.

Building Christian character is hard work—but it can be done in an enjoyable way, as *Max and the Big Fat Lie* points out.

Max's friend Stevie had just got a movie,
Slime Gobs from Space was its title.
"Get over here soon," Stevie phoned from his room.
"Cause seeing this movie is vital!"

Max wanted badly to see this great movie.
It was sure to be scary and loud.
But Mother and Dad would think it was bad
For movies like this weren't allowed!

Max did his best to think up a plan.
He thought 'til his eyeballs were sore.
And as he was thinking and painfully blinking
Somebody knocked on the door.

Max quickly jumped to his feet in surprise
For in through the door walked a fellow
Who was short as a stump, and equally plump—
What's more he was purple and yellow!

"Good day, my dear chap," said the short, purple creature.
"You're caught in a fix, I'll agree.
I can see on your face that *Slime Gobs from Space*
Is a movie you simply must see!"

"My name is Sir Fib and I think that you'll find
My services tend to be handy.
Please do not question, just take my suggestion:
A wee little fib would be dandy.

"Go tell your mother you're going to Stevie's,
But change the show's title a bit—
Pokey the Cow is a flick she'll allow.
Now go do your stuff—this is it!"

Of course, Max's mother was truly delighted—
Pokey the Cow would be swell!
It sounded so good, that if Stevie's mom could
The two moms might watch it as well.

9

This was a shocker to poor, little Max,
He hurried upstairs nearly crying.
If Mom came along the whole plan would go wrong
And Max would be punished for lying!

Sir Fib looked disturbed as he listened to Max.
He said, "This one's too big for me!
But I have a friend for whom I can send.
He'll know the answer, you'll see!"

So, he opened the door and he whistled a note.
It just took a second, not more,
For a tall lanky guy with a dark, shifty eye
To quickly slip through Max's door.

"Yo, Kid!" said the guy. "I'm Kleever Deceiver,
And Fib here has told me your story.
I've got what you need, and I think you'll agree
That deceiving should wipe out your worry!

"Go tell your ma that you just changed your mind
And you're gonna play baseball with Stevie.
She'll fall for the trick, then you go watch the flick.
It works every time, Kid, believe me."

Max hurried off with his new, improved lie,
Which Mother believed right away.
She showed not a doubt, but when Max turned about,
She had something awful to say.

"Since you'll be playing with Stevie Malone,"
Mom mentioned while feeding the cat,
"His mother and I could just visit awhile—
I've been meaning to stop for a chat!"

Max felt quite ill as he slithered upstairs
This was a problem indeed!
If Mother dropped by, he'd be caught in his lie
(Which was growing as fast as a weed!).

Kleever Deceiver turned terribly pale
When he heard about Mother's new plan.
"She's a foe I can't beat!" he cried in defeat.
"But I know a fellow who can!"

He leaned out the door, and peering both ways,
He called out "Hey yo! Big Fat Lie!"
And soon came a rumble, a thump, and a stumble
That felt like a train rolling by!

The creature was giant, all green and red-spotted,
It just barely squeezed through the door.
When it sat on the bed, the whole house shook instead,
And the mattress sank down to the floor.

"So this is the kid with the problem?" it said.
"A problem that I'll take away!
My name's Big Fat Lie, and I'll tell you why . . .
It's because I know just what to say!"

"Go tell your mother that Mrs. Malone
Has got the Mongolian Measles,
Their phone's disconnected, her toe is infected,
And the house was just treated for weasles.

"Tell her you'd much rather peddle your bike
Than have your mom give you a ride. . . .
Then she won't know where you boys really go—
Watching the *Slime Gobs* inside!"

Plodding his way down the stairs Max recited,
He practiced his new, big fat lie.
His kneecaps were shaking, his stomach was quaking,
But he had to give it a try.

"Mother," he said as he tried to stay calm,
"I fear that there's been complications. . . .
Mrs. Malone is no longer home,
She's gone off to visit relations.

"Their phone's disconnected, their poodle got sick,
And their house was attacked by a shark.
So, Stevie and I have just changed our minds—
We're going to ride bikes in the park."

Stevie had already set up the movie
By the time Max snuck up to his room.
They pulled down the shade and built a blockade,
And the room was as dark as a tomb.

Each time he heard talking or someone's shoes walking,
Max thought for sure he'd be caught.
He was in such a worry, the movie seemed blurry.
It wasn't such fun as he'd thought.

Max thought he felt someone's breath on his neck,
So he turned and he got a surprise.
It was Sir Fib and Kleever, that clever Deceiver,
But the breath that he felt was the Lie's.

After a while he could take it no more,
He jumped to his feet in a panic!
He raced his bike home, but he wasn't alone,
For the weight on his bike was titanic!

On the back of his bike were Sir Fib and Deceiver
And heavier still was the Lie.
"Whatever you do," said the Lie turning blue,
"Don't look your mom in the eye!

"Tell her that you were attacked by a tiger
And trapped in a telephone booth. . . .
The Martians invaded! The planet was raided!
Just make sure you don't tell the truth!"

"Get lost!" shouted Max. "I don't need all your lies,
The truth will work just fine for me.
I'm finished with lying and sneaking and spying—
So you guys just might as well leave!"

At that very moment, in one mighty flash,
The Lie and his friends disappeared.
Max felt more relieved than you could've believed . . .
For now Max's conscience was cleared.

28

Max told his mom of the lies he'd made up,
How he'd been sneaky and bad.
He said he was sorry, and she needn't worry—
He learned from the lesson he'd had.

Mom never did let Max go see the *Slime Gobs*
Though once in a while he still taunts her.
But Max doesn't lie, and we all know why—
A lie's like a big, ugly monster!

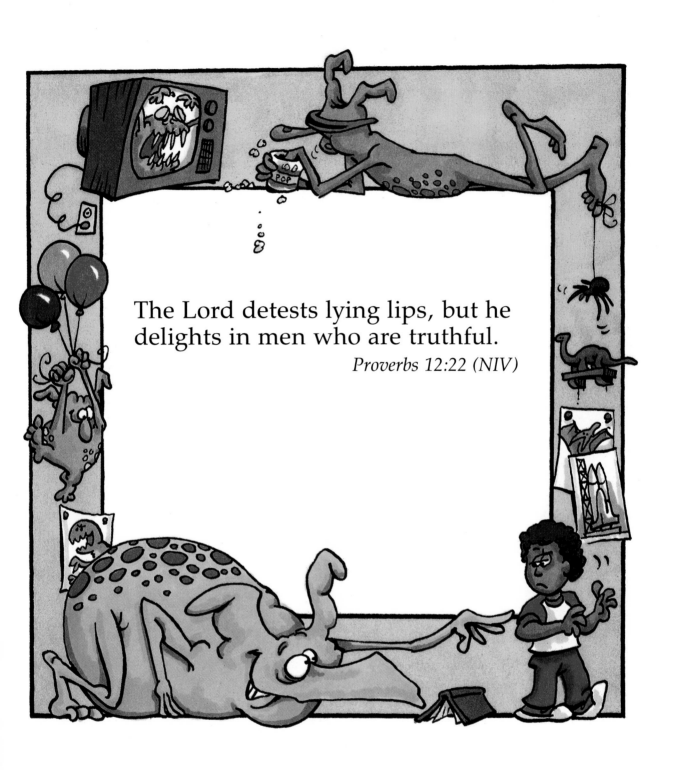

The Lord detests lying lips, but he delights in men who are truthful.

Proverbs 12:22 (NIV)

Look for all the great stories in the
Building Christian Character series

Buzzle Billy—A Book About Sharing
Handy-Dandy Helpful Hal—A Book About Helpfulness
Miggy and Tiggy—A Book About Overcoming Jealousy
Suzy Swoof—A Book About Kindness
Max and the Big Fat Lie—A Book About Telling the Truth
Casey the Greedy Young Cowboy—A Book About Being Thankful
Sir Maggie the Mighty—A Book About Obedience
Boggin, Blizzy, and Sleeter the Cheater—A Book About Fairness